BIG BAD
DETECTIVE AGENCY

BRUCE HALE

SCHOLASTIC INC.

No part of this publication may be reproduced, stored in a retrieval system, or transmitted in any form or by any means, electronic, mechanical, photocopying, recording, or otherwise, without written permission of the publisher. For information regarding permission, write to Scholastic Inc., Attention: Permissions Department, 557 Broadway, New York, NY 10012.

ISBN 978-0-545-66538-4

10 9 8 7 6 5 4 3 2 1   15 16 17 18 19 20/0

Printed in the U.S.A.   40
First printing, February 2015
Book design by Yaffa Jaskoll

To Claudotte Brown and her kids of renown

CHAPTER 1

In which a wolf faces death by porridge

Once upon a time in Fairylandia, when magic was common and cheese was two shillings a pound, there lived a wolf named Wolfgang. Being a wolf, he was widely adored, called "cute" and "cuddly," and invited to all the best parties.

Not.

What makes you think Fairylandia is so different from anyplace else? In truth, most of its citizens avoided him, feared him, and called him "Big Bad Wolf." This was hardly fair. Sure, he was large and scary-looking, and yes, he'd stolen a few chickens (okay, a *lot* of chickens) here and there. But Wolfgang was really making an effort to reform himself and get his new gardening business off the ground.

Did anyone care? They did not.

So it comes as no surprise, then, that when someone trashed the Three Little Pigs' houses, the prince's guards arrested Wolfgang. They dragged him from his simple home up to the grand throne room, with its marble floors, graceful arches, and vaulted ceiling. But the wolf had other things than architecture on his mind.

"I'm innocent" were the first words from Wolfgang's mouth.

"*Innocent?*" Prince Tyrone chuckled. "Impossible. You're a wolf."

Wolfgang growled, which really didn't help matters. "Let me rephrase that," he said. "I didn't do it."

"Of course you did," said the handsome Prince Tyrone, smoothing his hair. "I'm certain you did it, therefore you did it."

"I was home reading a gardening book last night," said Wolfgang. "Where's your proof?"

"My guards found wolf prints on the path that runs by one of the pigs' houses," the prince said.

"Maybe because that path also leads to *my* house," Wolfgang said.

"Don't let him trick you, Highness," said Captain Kreplach, commander of the guards. "Wolves is mighty tricksy, they is."

With an effort, Wolfgang controlled his temper. "Did you find any evidence *inside* the pigs' homes?" he asked.

The prince looked at the captain. The captain looked at the wolf.

"Well, no," said Captain Kreplach. "But that's 'cause you're so tricksy."

Wolfgang rolled his eyes.

"That's him, Your Excellency," a grunty voice declared. "He's the one."

The wolf turned to see the Three Little Pigs

pushing aside the tapestries and emerging from a side room. Dieter, the biggest pig, was pointing directly at him.

A word about the Three Little Pigs. Full-grown, well-fed porkers, they were anything *but* little. Dieter, Martin, and Hans ran PorkerBuilt, a successful construction company, which put enough food on the table to make them the Three Ginormous Pigs.

But nicknames in Fairylandia, once given, tend to stick.

"He wrecked our homes and stole our food," said Martin, the second-biggest pig.

Wolfgang snarled. Martin jumped back, bumping into Hans.

"I didn't trash your silly houses," said the wolf. "In fact, I want nothing to do with you."

Except in the form of pork chops, thought Wolfgang. He'd been dragged away from breakfast, after all, and his stomach was grumbling. Plus, these bothersome pigs were always accusing him of one thing or another, and he'd had just about enough of it.

"Oh yeah?" said Dieter, feeling brave with the guards in the room.

"*Yeah,*" the wolf growled.

Dieter jumped back, bumping into Martin. All three pigs went down like chubby bowling pins.

Hans spoke up from the floor. "If you want nothing to do with us, how come you're always pounding on our door at night?"

"Because your music's too loud," said Wolfgang. "I can't stand that racket."

Being a not-too-distant neighbor of Dieter's, the wolf often heard them playing oompah music. Or trying to, anyway. Wolfgang loved a good tune, but to be perfectly honest, their playing was more *oom-blah* than *oom-pah*.

Martin jabbed a stubby hoof at Wolfgang. "See? That's why he did it. Music hater!"

Dieter appealed to Prince Tyrone. "Please, Sire, chop off his head? Have some witch turn him into a newt?"

The prince's eyes narrowed. "First, don't call me 'Sire.' 'Sire' is for kings."

Dieter frowned. "But it's the *Kingdom* of Fairylandia."

"Yes, I know," said Prince Tyrone through gritted teeth.

"Kingdoms are usually ruled by kings."

"That's . . . true." A tic had developed in the prince's right eyelid.

"So," said the biggest pig, "why aren't you a king?"

Prince Tyrone's face turned scarlet. His eyelid twitched so fiercely, it looked like he was trying to wink in Morse code. "I. Don't. Know," he said. "And it drives . . . me . . . *CRAZY!*"

He pounded his fists on the throne's arms.

Princess Ingrid rushed up to her husband, took his hand, and helped him from the chair. Murmuring soft words, she led Prince Tyrone away.

"But, Si — er, Your Highness," squeaked Hans. "The wolf must be punished!"

"For the last time, I DIDN'T DO IT!" bellowed Wolfgang. The guards flinched.

Princess Ingrid addressed Captain Kreplach. "The prince is unwell. Will you handle this, Captain?"

The burly commander snapped to attention. "Count on me, Your Majes — um, Highness."

With a frosty look, the princess led her griping husband off to their chambers. Wolfgang didn't know whether her turning matters over to the captain was a good thing or a bad thing. He soon found out.

"Right, then." Captain Kreplach fixed a glare on the three pigs. "You," he snapped. "Stop your whinin'. Nothin' I hates more than whinin' — 'cept maybe blubberin'."

"Captain —" the wolf began.

"And *you*," the captain said. "What do I do with you?"

Wolfgang smiled a toothy smile. Several guards gasped. "Let me go?" he said.

Captain Kreplach gnawed on a piece of his massive mustache. "Hmm . . . it's true we gots no evidence."

"But he's a *wolf*," whined Martin Pig.

The captain held up a hand. "What did I just say about whinin'?"

"You, um, hates it?" said Martin in a small voice.

"Good boy." Captain Kreplach paced before the throne, musing. "We gots no proof, but then again, we gots no suspects 'cept the Big Bad Wolf."

"I hate that name," Wolfgang rumbled.

"Tough tootsies," said the captain. "Now, if you, Mr. Bad —"

"Mr. Wolf," the wolf corrected.

"— were to catch the real culprit, I might just let you off the hook."

Wolfgang gaped. "Me? Catch a culprit?"

"Yes, of course. Who else?"

The wolf looked from the soldiers back to the captain. "Well, *you*," he said. "You *are* the prince's guards, aren't you?"

"Too right." Captain Kreplach gestured at his troops. "And we've got our hands full with guardin'. Nothin' but guardin', day in, day out."

His men nodded. "You tell 'em, Cap'n," said one.

"So you see," said Captain Kreplach, "it's up to you, Wolf."

Wolfgang scowled. "And if I refuse?"

"Into the dungeon with you," said Captain Kreplach.

"Just because I'm a wolf?" said Wolfgang, his voice dangerously quiet.

The captain nodded. "Just because."

"That's not fair!"

A dry chuckle escaped the captain's lips. "Don't let the name Fairylandia fool you, mate. Life ain't fair. But, seein' as how I'm a generous man, you've got till sundown to bring me the culprit."

"And if I fail?"

Captain Kreplach's smile was a fearsome thing. "You'll spend your life in a dungeon, eatin' porridge."

Wolfgang blanched. "No deer?"

"No deer," said Kreplach.

"No rabbit?"

"No rabbit," said the captain.

"Not even mouse?" asked the wolf.

"Not even a cockroach."

"Porridge." Wolfgang shuddered. "I *hate* porridge."

"Then you'd best get crackin'," said Captain Kreplach.

The wolf pushed aside his guards, nodded

at the captain, and with one last scowl at the Three Little Pigs, stalked from the throne room.

One day to find the criminal, or face death by porridge. Wolfgang shook his shaggy head grimly.

He could almost feel the iron bars closing in around him. It was not a good feeling.

CHAPTER 2

In which pigs snarl and mops attack

Before we continue, a word about Fairylandia. It was not, as some suppose, a land of milk and honey where bluebirds sang all day and pixies did your housework. Far from it.

Like anywhere else, Fairylandia had its fair share of problems. Witches were forever turning people into toads and then refusing to turn them back. Giants accidentally stepped on houses, and you couldn't get insurance to cover the damage.

And don't even get me started on the magic goose poop.

In short, the fairy tales you've heard were a bit off the mark. Heroes were not entirely good, and villains? In some cases they were just misunderstood.

And speaking of misunderstood villains, let's return to Wolfgang.

The wolf stomped out of the castle, seething. Who was he, a top predator on the food chain and a talented gardener, to be threatened by some fuzzy-lipped punk like Captain Kreplach? Especially when he was innocent! It positively burned his butt.

"Not fair!" he howled.

But Kreplach was the prince's enforcer, and Wolfgang, like it or not, was under Prince Tyrone's rule. So the wolf contented himself with kicking a fence, scaring some townsfolk, and knocking down a mailbox.

Tantrum over, he sat on a boulder to brood.

First thought: Eat Captain Kreplach. No, that wouldn't work. The prince would only send more guards, and besides, the captain would make a mighty gristly meal.

Second thought: Leave Fairylandia. No, his family had lived here for ages, and Wolfgang would be double-dog-danged if he'd slip out with his tail between his legs.

Third thought: Find the culprit.

Hmm . . .

The wolf *was* a hunter, after all. He trotted on down the road to Dieter Pig's place to pick up the housebreaker's scent.

As Wolfgang approached the brick house, his keen sniffer was struck by a dreadful stench: ammonia, lemony polish, and all kinds of cleaning products. A cheery, off-key whistling pierced his furry ears.

Someone was in the house!

The culprit had returned to cover his tracks. The wolf's tail wagged. Could it really be this easy?

Fangs bared, Wolfgang rushed up the walkway and flung open the door.

"Aha!" he cried. "Back at the scene of the crime!"

A stout sow in an apron turned from her work, wet mop in hand.

"You!" she gasped.

"You?" said Wolfgang. He frowned. "*You're* the housebreaker?"

The sow's eyes narrowed to slits. "I'm the what, now?"

Wolfgang felt a little less sure. "The one who . . . um, broke into your sons' houses, trashed them, and stole all the food?"

Her mop rose like a club as Mama Pig advanced.

"You've got a lot of nerve, mister," she snarled. Wolfgang had never heard a pig snarl before.

"Thanks," he said, taking a casual step back. "I was voted nerviest wolf in my pack."

"How dare you accuse me?" Mama Pig demanded. "You, the real criminal? I should beat you like a Persian rug!"

She swung the mop, and Wolfgang ducked. Dirty water sprayed over his back. Mama Pig swung again, and the wolf dodged out the door.

"I'm innocent," he growled.

"Hah!"

"Okay, okay. I mean, I didn't do it. I was home with a good book." Was his reputation that bad? he wondered. He really had to get out more, let people see the *real* Wolfgang. This constant mistrust was getting old.

The sow glared at him. She had a pretty good glare, for a pig.

"I hope they lock you up and throw away the key," said Mama Pig, jabbing the mop into his gut.

Wolfgang stumbled back. "I'm just trying to find out who really did this to your —"

BAM! The door slammed shut.

"— rotten little oinkers," the wolf finished.

Two locks clicked into place. "And stay out!" cried Mama Pig.

Wolfgang snarled and snapped, but the door stayed closed. Grumbling and growling, he stalked back down the walkway.

What now? he wondered. Eat Mama Pig? Tempting, but then he'd be in even more hot water than he was already.

"*Psst*, hey!" said a squeaky voice.

Wolfgang glanced behind him. Nobody there.

"Down here," said the voice.

The wolf looked down. Standing on the path before him was a tiny pink pig, no higher than his waist, wearing a blue felt cap.

"What now?" Wolfgang barked. He had more than enough pigs in his life already, thanks very much.

The porker grinned. "I'm Ferkel."

"And I'm history if I don't catch that thief. See ya." He started off.

"Wait!" cried the pig. "I can help you. I can! I'm cheerful, good with people, and I always wanted to be a detective."

"A what?" rumbled Wolfgang, tramping down the path as Ferkel trotted to keep up.

"A detective. That's what I call people who solve mysteries. I love mysteries, don't you?"

"No," said the wolf.

"But —"

"And even if I did, I don't need your help. Later, short stuff." Wolfgang lengthened his stride.

"Wait!" the pig cried. "I've already got a clue!"

The wolf stopped so short, Ferkel ran right into him.

"What clue?" Wolfgang asked.

The pig gave a coy smile. "Promise first?"

Wolfgang scowled. "Promise what?"

"That you'll let me help you solve the mystery of what happened to my brothers' houses."

"Wait, you're related to those three trouble-makers?" The wolf didn't know if this was a good thing or a bad thing. But the way his luck had been lately, it was probably bad.

"Sure am," said Ferkel. "I've been living at home with my mama, but she said I can leave if I find a job — like detecting. So . . . promise?"

Their gazes locked. The wolf glared, but the
pig gazed right back. Wolfgang blinked first.

"Oh, all right," he grumbled. "You can help.
What's the clue?"

Ferkel reached under his cap and produced a
brown-and-red head scarf.

"Ta-da!"

"*That's* your clue?" Wolfgang asked.

Ferkel nodded vigorously. "I found it in the bushes. It looks familiar, but then, it's a common style. I think the thief dropped it."

Wolfgang sniffed. The scarf smelled, unsurprisingly, of pig. Big help.

"Great," he said. "Dust your furniture with it."

"Don't you see?" said Ferkel. "We draw up a list of suspects, interview them, and find out if anyone is missing a scarf."

"Too much like work," said Wolfgang. "I'll just follow my nose, like always."

"*Ferrrr-kellll!*" Mama Pig's voice echoed down the road. "Where are you?"

The little porker tucked the scarf back under his cap. "Gotta go. Meet you in a half hour at Hansel and Gretel's place."

"Why there?"

Ferkel made a *duh* face. "Hansel and Gretel? Notorious housebreakers? Keep up, Wolfie!"

Wolfgang growled, "Don't call me Wolfie."

But the little pig had scurried off.

CHAPTER 3

In which nobody is turned into a newt

A half hour later, Wolfgang stood at the edge of the sun-dappled woods by Hansel and Gretel's house. Right on time, up trotted Ferkel.

"Ready to start our first case?" said the little pig.

"Our?" said the wolf. *"First?"*

Ferkel grinned. "I have a good feeling. This is the start of something big!"

"Yeah? So is the snowball that becomes an avalanche," muttered Wolfgang darkly.

Nevertheless, the wolf led the way across the lawn and up to Hansel and Gretel's cozy cabin.

A word about H & G, before we meet them. If you've heard their story, you probably think they were a pair of sweet kids who narrowly missed being gobbled up by a mean old witch.

Yeah. Not quite.

In truth, H & G were greedy, ruthless teenage twins who had started up their own sweets shop. One dark night, they'd entirely devoured their competition, Ursula's Goodies, literally eating poor Ursula the Witch out of house and home and eliminating all her stock. In their free time, they enjoyed a bit of petty thievery.

Wolfgang rapped on the stout green door.

"Who is it?" a surly girl's voice demanded.

The wolf started to answer, then stopped short. This called for a little tricksiness — which was, in fact, a specialty of his. Much as he wanted to reform his image, reform would have to wait.

His own voice went all high and innocent. "I'm collecting for charity."

"Beat it," said someone else, probably Hansel.

"We've got candy," sang Ferkel.

Whfff! The door whipped open.

"What kind do —?" Hansel began, until he saw who stood on his doorstep. "You? Get lost!"

The blond boy tried to slam the door, but Wolfgang had jammed his paw into the frame.

"We only want — *ow!* — to talk," the wolf said.

Gretel's head peeked over her brother's shoulder. "Where's the candy?"

"There is none!" Ferkel chuckled. "We just wanted you to open up."

Hansel and Gretel shoved on the door. Wolfgang braced his shoulder against them, trying to spare his mashed paw.

"Where — *ugh* — were you last night?" asked the wolf.

"None of your — *mmf!* — beeswax," said Hansel. His round belly poked through the gap as he struggled in vain to close the door.

"We were right here," said Gretel, "doing a taste test between chocolate, vanilla, and coconut cakes."

"Ooh! Which one won?" asked Ferkel.

Gretel's smile was dreamy. "All of 'em. We're doing pies tomorrow."

"Big whoop," Wolfgang growled. "Tell me, what do you think of the Three Little Pigs?"

"Those oinkers?" Hansel snapped. "Hate 'em. Hate their building projects, too. Keep the forest green, I say!"

Gretel produced a rolling pin from somewhere and poked it in Wolfgang's eye. When he stepped back, clapping a paw over the injury, the twins slammed and locked the door.

"Ow!" cried the wolf. "Open up!"

"Never!" cried H & G.

"Open that dog-danged door," barked the wolf. "Or I'll huff, and I'll puff, and I'll blow it right down!"

A moment of silence followed this threat. Then . . .

"Ha, ha, ha, ha!" The twins burst into hysterical laughter.

"I'm not kidding," said Wolfgang. "I'll do it — see if I don't!"

More laughter.

Ferkel frowned. "Can you really blow a door down?" he whispered.

"Don't be ridiculous," said the wolf. "What do I look like, a tornado?" He headed off across the lawn.

"Ooh! Where are we going?" asked the pig, trotting after him.

"To find something vitally important to this investigation."

"What's that?" asked Ferkel. "Another clue?"

The wolf smiled a hungry smile. "Lunch," he said.

Of all the restaurants in Fairylandia, the Hi-Ho Diner was the most popular. It was also the only one. Snow White ran the place with a firm hand, bossing around her staff of seven dwarfs and dishing up the best burgers, shakes, and dragon-egg omelets in town.

Wolfgang and Ferkel strode into the warm, bustling restaurant, which smelled of fresh-baked bread and dwarf sweat. After the pair had placed their order, they sat back in a red leather booth to discuss their first suspects.

"We didn't get to see if they recognized that head scarf," said Ferkel. "But I don't think they did it."

"Are you kidding?" said Wolfgang. "They hate your brothers, they have no alibi but each other, and they acted suspicious."

Ferkel raised his eyebrows. "Suspicious? You lied about candy and threatened to blow down their house. How else would they act?"

"*You* lied about the candy," grumped the wolf. "Anyway, I still think Hansel and Gretel are guilty."

"Oh, they *are*," rasped a scratchy voice behind them.

Wolfgang spun in his seat to eyeball a lean, black-clad woman at the next booth. "You have proof?" he asked.

She nodded glumly. "Hansel and Gretel ate my home — what more do you need?"

"Um, proof that they trashed my brothers'
houses?" said Ferkel.

The wolf frowned at the woman. "You're
Ursula?"

"The witch?" said Ferkel with a gulp.

"The same," said Ursula, plucking a wing
from her bat soup.

Ferkel shrank back. "Didn't you sue my

brothers because they built your house from gingerbread?"

"Well, yeah," said the witch. "I mean, who builds a house from snack food? It was a pain to keep clean, and then those rotten kids ate the whole thing up."

Wolfgang's eyes narrowed. "So you don't much like the Three Little Pigs?"

Ursula shot him a deadpan look. "What do you think, handsome?"

"I think you better tell us where you were last night," growled the wolf. His hackles bristled.

Ferkel tugged on his arm. "Don't make her mad," he whispered. "She'll turn us into newts."

Wolfgang shook him off. "Where were you, witchy woman?" he demanded.

Plates slammed onto their table. "With me," snapped the sour-looking dwarf serving their food. "Isn't that right, Love Muffin?"

Ursula beamed at the grim little man. "That's right, Schnooky Lumps. We went to hear that new harpist play at the castle."

Wolfgang slumped. "So you didn't wreck the pigs' houses?"

She stood and linked her arm with the dwarf's. "It makes me happy to hear it," she said. "But no, I didn't. Try Jack — he's a known thief and rascal."

"Right." Wolfgang waved a paw in thanks and tucked into his meal: four griffin burgers with a side of venison and fries. It might be his last meal that didn't consist of porridge.

As she passed by, Ursula trailed her fingers

over Ferkel's shoulder. "Oh, and, Little Pig?" she said.

"Yes?" said Ferkel.

"Nobody turns anybody into newts these days."

Ferkel blushed and seemed to relax.

"The best witches turn folks into wombats."

And with a light cackle, she left the diner.

CHAPTER 4

In which a pig gets tricksy

Jack lived on a tumbledown farm with his mother, a mangy cow, and a few fat hens. Since the lad was, as Ursula had noted, a well-known rascal, Wolfgang felt hopeful. He and Ferkel approached the cottage.

"Now can we use my investigative techniques?" asked Ferkel.

"Maybe next time," said Wolfgang. He rapped on the cottage door.

"Who is it?" a young man's voice called.

"Wolfgang," said the wolf.

"And me, Ferkel," the pig added.

"The Big Bad Wolf and the Little Bitty Pig?" said the voice.

Wolfgang grimaced. "Don't call me 'Big Bad.' Open up, Jack."

"Ma always said don't talk to strangers," said Jack.

"We're not strangers," Wolfgang growled. "You know us. Now, open up!"

A thumping and dragging noise came from inside. "Fair point," said Jack. "But a guy can't be too careful these days."

The weathered door creaked open just a

smidgen and a wary blue eye peeked through the crack. "Hullo," said Jack.

"Hi," said Ferkel. "How's it going?"

Wolfgang turned to stare. "'How's it going?' *That's* your investigative technique?"

Ferkel shrugged. "No harm in being polite."

The wolf ground his teeth. "There is if you're facing death by porridge."

"Fine." Ferkel threw up his hooves. "Do it your way."

"Do what?" asked Jack.

Wolfgang cleared his throat. "Have you had any doings with the Three Little Pigs?"

The door opened just wide enough to reveal Jack's other eye. "Seen 'em around once or twice," said Jack. "You know."

"How do you get along?" asked Wolfgang.

"I've got no beef with the pigs," said Jack. He gave them an expectant grin. "Get it? *Beef* with pigs?"

Wolfgang rolled his eyes. "Hilarious. Recognize this head scarf?" He held up the brown and red fabric.

"Nope," said Jack.

"Where were you last night?" the wolf demanded.

The door gap narrowed. "Why so many questions?"

"Someone vandalized my brothers' houses while they were off listening to that new harpist," Ferkel piped up.

"And I'm getting really curious about what you're hiding behind that door," Wolfgang snarled, shouldering his way through. "Now, open *up!*"

BAM! The door flew open. Jack stumbled backward and landed flat on his hot cross buns.

And Wolfgang and Ferkel saw what the door had been hiding:

A small stack of brass eggs, a pair of crutches, and a leg — Jack's leg — in a plaster cast.

Wolfgang frowned at the broken leg. "Huh?"

"I, uh, fell out of a tree last week," said Jack.

"And the eggs?" asked Ferkel.

Jack shrugged. "Bought 'em off a stranger."

"So, last night . . . ?" Wolfgang said.

"I was right here at home," said Jack. "With Ma."

Wolfgang's tail drooped. "Oh." He turned to go. "Right."

"Wait a second," said Ferkel. "You got the eggs from a stranger? You said your mom told you never to talk to strangers."

"Yup." Jack gave a wry headshake. "And that's why she told me that."

Back outside, Wolfgang pulled on his ears in frustration. "Only five hours till sundown, and we haven't caught the culprit yet."

"*Now* will you try my investigative techniques?" said Ferkel.

Wolfgang sighed. "Will they keep me out of the dungeon?"

Ferkel chuckled and rubbed his front hooves together. "Absolutely! First thing we do is create a list of suspects."

They strolled along the forest road, adding and discarding names, until at last they had a fair list.

"All right," said Wolfgang. "Read off the new ones."

"Goldilocks."

"Check."

"Cinderella," said Ferkel.

"Check."

"Thumbelina."

"Really?" Wolfgang arched an eyebrow. "She's smaller than a thumb."

Ferkel shrugged. "She'd have an easy time breaking in."

"Uh-huh. And how would she steal all that food?"

Ferkel crossed off the name. "Okay, no Thumbelina."

"Right," said Wolfgang, lengthening his stride. "Let's go."

"Where?"

"First, Goldilocks," said the wolf. "I've never trusted blondes."

A word about Goldilocks before we meet her. As you may know, young miss Goldie had a rather free attitude toward other people's belongings.

Eating other people's oatmeal, sleeping in their beds, and trying on their clothes didn't make her the most popular of girls. Plus, because of her experience with the Three Bears, she was a wee bit shy around big predators — a fact that Ferkel pointed out.

"You can't just go barging in there," he said.

"Why not?" said Wolfgang.

"Well, you're a wolf."

Wolfgang stopped, looked down at himself,

and then back at the pig. "My, you *are* a detective," he said. "So?"

"She'll never open the door."

The wolf put his paws on his hips. "And what
do you suggest? Climbing down her chimney?"

"A real detective would get tricksy," said
Ferkel. "A real detective would wear a disguise."

Wolfgang eyed the pig. "Exactly what did
you have in mind?"

CHAPTER 5

In which the world's ugliest granny comes to call

No way," said Wolfgang. "Never in a million years!"

"It's genius!" said Ferkel. He held up the flowery flannel nightgown and mobcap he'd borrowed from his mother. "It'll make you look harmless. Well, more harmless, anyway."

The wolf glared. "Are you cracked? I've got a reputation."

"Everyone fears and mistrusts you."

Wolfgang shrugged. "It may be a bad reputation, but it's a reputation. What if someone sees me wearing granny clothes?"

Ferkel stepped closer. "You want to stay out of Prince Tyrone's dungeon, right?"

"Of course, but —"

"And you want to question Goldilocks, right?"

Wolfgang grimaced. "Yeah, but —"

"Do you have any better ideas," Ferkel said innocently, "for making Goldilocks trust the Big Bad Wolf?"

Wolfgang scowled at him for a beat. At last, he snatched the nightgown from Ferkel and growled, "If you *ever* tell anyone about this, you're bacon bits. Got that?"

Ferkel smiled. "You're welcome. Don't forget the cap!"

Wolfgang stepped behind some bushes and slipped into the gown, tucking his ears under the frilly mobcap. After some tweaking and tugging, he stepped out again.

"I feel like an idiot," he said.

Ferkel cocked his head this way and that. "Don't take this the wrong way," he said, "but you look like the world's ugliest granny."

"Funny, Pig. Real funny."

"It needs . . . something," said Ferkel. "Bend down."

When Wolfgang stooped, the pig tugged the nightcap as low as it would go. Then he patted the wolf's furry face with a powder puff and smeared some red lipstick across his snout.

"That's it," said Ferkel. "Let's hear your granny voice?"

"Hello, little girl," growled the wolf in a voice like boulders rumbling.

Ferkel winced. "Leave the talking to me."

Wolfgang gnashed his teeth. This day just couldn't get much worse. Nevertheless, he followed Ferkel down the path.

Goldilocks lived in a cozy little thatch-roofed cottage beside a grove of apple trees. Scattered about the yard were various chairs, beds, tables, meals, and bits of clothing, both large and small.

Wolfgang sniffed at a chair as they passed by. "She's a tidy little thing," he muttered.

"I hear she's really picky," Ferkel whispered. "Everything has to be just right."

"Except for her housekeeping, apparently," said the wolf.

They knocked on the door but got no answer. Then Wolfgang's sharp ears detected a cheerful whistling coming from the orchard. Strolling around the side of the cottage, they spotted a sturdy blond teenager skipping toward them, carrying a basket of apples.

"Hello there!" said Ferkel. "Beautiful day, isn't it?"

"Oh!" The girl stopped dead, brown eyes round with surprise. "Who are you?"

The pig swept off his blue cap and made a gallant bow. "Ferkel Pig, at your service."

Her gaze went from him to Wolfgang. "And who's your ugly friend?"

The wolf started to growl, but Ferkel elbowed him into silence.

"He — uh, *she's* called . . ." the pig began.

"Lobo," said the wolf.

"Granny Goodie," said Ferkel at the same time.

Goldilocks frowned. "Well, which is it?"

The wolf attempted the world's most awkward curtsy. "Granny Lobo Goodie, my dear," he rumbled, then caught himself. "Pleased to meet you," he squeaked.

Goldilocks hugged her basket closer and cast him a doubtful look. "Charmed," she said. "I just love your fashion sense."

"What do you mean?" asked Ferkel.

"Not every woman is bold enough to wear nightclothes in the middle of the day," she said.

Wolfgang shot the pig a glare.

"Er, yes," said Ferkel. "Granny's a bold one, all right."

Goldilocks edged around them toward the house. "What do you want?"

"Oh, just a neighborly gossip session," said Ferkel. "Did you hear what happened to the Three Little Pigs last night?"

"Yes," said Goldie, keeping her distance.

"What a shame. I heard they had to move back in with their mother."

"Who do you think did it?" Ferkel asked.

"No idea," said the girl, with a nervous glance at Wolfgang.

He smiled reassuringly, his sharp fangs glinting.

"Wow!" said Goldilocks. "Those are some seriously big teeth you've got."

Ferkel scowled at Wolfgang.

"The better to, uh, eat . . . my porridge with," screeched the wolf in his best try at a female voice.

"Riiiight," said the girl. By now, she'd gotten around them and was backing toward the house.

Following after, Wolfgang drew the head scarf from inside his sleeve. "We found this on the ground, dearie. You didn't happen to drop it, did you?"

Her eyes flashed from the scarf back to the wolf's face. "Not mine," she said.

Just then, Wolfgang felt a terrible urge to scratch underneath the mobcap. He raised a paw and gave the itchy spot a quick *scritch-scritch-scritch*. But as he did so, his ears popped free.

"Yikes, what big ears you have!" said Goldie in a small voice.

"Uh, yes," the wolf trilled. "I, uh — ah, forget it." His voice dropped back into its normal register. "The better to hear you say what the heck you were doing last night between sunset and midnight."

Goldilocks turned and fled for her cottage

door. Wolfgang lunged after her, tangled his legs in the nightgown, and did a face-plant into her tomato garden. He raised a red-stained muzzle and cried, "Stop her!"

Ferkel trotted as fast as his little trotters would carry him, just managing to reach the door before Goldie. He spread his arms across the doorframe. "Wait, we —" he began.

"Move it, Pig!" The girl caught Ferkel's shoulder and flung him aside, in a move worthy of judo, which hadn't even been invented yet.

The pig just managed to grab her ankle as she barreled through the doorway.

Wolfgang regained his feet and surged forward.

"Help!" cried Goldilocks. "Someone save me!"

The three of them grappled on the doorstep,

Goldie trying to escape, Ferkel and Wolfgang trying to explain.

FWEEEET! A shrill whistle blast pierced the air.

"Ho there!" bellowed a rough voice. "Halt, in the name of the prince!"

CHAPTER 6

In which a wolf gets fashion tips

Captain Kreplach marched up the walkway with two tall guards at his heels. "Unhand her!" he cried. Wolfgang and Ferkel released Goldilocks, who promptly swatted them with her basket.

"It's not what it looks like," said Wolfgang.

"I'll be the judge of that, madam," snapped

Captain Kreplach. He stopped and squinted suspiciously. "Hang on. Don't I know you?"

The wolf brought a paw up to his muzzle and avoided the captain's eyes. "No," he squeaked. "Never had the pleasure."

Kreplach pulled on his mustache. "I never forgets a face, 'specially one as unfortunate as yours. No offense, madam."

"None taken," trilled Wolfgang. "It's all a simple misunderstanding." Head down, he tried to slip around the guards.

"Stop him!" cried Goldilocks.

The two soldiers blocked Wolfgang's retreat.

"'Him'?" Captain Kreplach repeated, peering at the wolf's face. "Don't you mean —?" His jaw dropped. "Strike me silly. Is that . . . the Big Bad Wolf?"

"Don't call me that!" barked the wolf.

The captain snorted a laugh. "Wolfgang? All dressed up like a granny? Ha! Now I've seen everything."

The guards chuckled and nudged each other.

Wolfgang scowled. If he hadn't been so furry, he would've blushed redder than a sunset. "All right now," he said. "It's not *that* funny."

The older guard cackled. "The roughest bruiser in the — *ha! ha! ha!* — forest. And he's wearing — *hee, hee!* — makeup!"

"That's enough," growled Wolfgang.

"And not very well, either," said the second guard. "Maybe he should get makeup tips from Snow White!" They broke into gales of laughter.

The wolf glowered at Ferkel. "This is all your fault."

The pig shrugged. "Sorry."

"Hey!" cried Goldilocks. "This freak and his pet porker attack me, and all you do is laugh?"

Captain Kreplach and his guards made an effort to simmer down.

"Right, then," he said. "Tell us what happened, miss."

Goldilocks elbowed Ferkel aside. "I was just minding my own business, picking apples, see?" she said. "Of course you need to make sure they're not too big, not too small; not too ripe, not too unripe; not too tart, not too —"

"Yeah, yeah, just right," said the captain, who knew of Goldie's reputation. "Go on."

"I was returning to the house, when these two wackos started asking questions. When I tried to go, they attacked me." She glared at Wolfgang.

"Not true!" said the wolf.

"You did ask some weird questions," said Goldilocks.

"I was only trying to find out who trashed the Three Pigs' houses," he said, appealing to the captain.

Goldie put a hand on her hip, eyes narrowing. "And you thought *I* did it?"

"You *are* a notorious housebreaker," said Wolfgang.

She whacked him with her basket again, sending apples flying. "Take that back, you weirdo wolf!"

"Here now, miss!" said the captain. "Settle down."

"You see?" said Wolfgang. "Rude and uncooperative. Guilty for sure!"

Captain Kreplach frowned. "You — first off, lose that cap. It's creepy."

The wolf growled, but he whipped off the cap and wiped off his makeup with it.

"Now, Miss Goldie," said the captain. "If you'll just answer a simple question, we can all be on our way."

"What's that?" she asked.

Ferkel cut in. "Where were you last night between sunset and midnight?"

"Button it." Captain Kreplach sent him an exasperated look, then turned to the girl. "Yeah, what the pig said."

"*Me?*" Goldilocks drew herself up. "I'm not the guilty one here. These beasts attacked me on my own —"

"Answer the dog-danged question!" snarled Wolfgang.

Goldie stepped back, eyes wide. "Oh my. Well, um, last night I was having a slumber party."

"Can anyone confirm that?" asked Ferkel.

The captain glared at him again. "Stop doin' my job, pig." He turned to the girl. "Can anyone confirm that?"

Goldilocks huffed, but she answered. "Rapunzel and Thumbelina. We were up all night, braiding Rapunzel's hair, and we almost lost Thumbelina in it. Just ask her, if you don't believe me."

"Maybe we will," Wolfgang sneered.

"Thanks, miss," said Captain Kreplach. "We're done here."

"But aren't you going to punish the wolf?" She pouted.

The captain eyed Wolfgang. "He'll get

punishment enough, if he don't find the culprit by sundown."

Goldie flounced inside and slammed the door.

Captain Kreplach leaned close to the wolf and whispered three words: "Porridge. For. Life."

Wolfgang flinched.

The captain swaggered back down the walk after his men. At the gate, he turned.

"You know . . ." he began.

"What?" said the wolf.

"Next time you wear a nightie, try somethin' in ivory. Pink just ain't your color."

With a mean laugh, the guards marched away.

The wolf cocked a worried eye at the sun slanting through the pines. "Only three hours left," he said, "and we're running out of suspects."

CHAPTER 7

In which someone gets a serious licking

As Ferkel and Wolfgang tramped on down the forest road, the wolf growled, "This detective stuff isn't working out."

Ferkel waved away his comment. "Don't be so negative, Mr. Grumpy-pants."

Grumpy-pants? thought Wolfgang.

"Here's what we do now," said Ferkel. "Look for more clues at the scene of the crime."

The wolf ducked under a low-hanging branch. "But we already saw the brick house — nothing there."

"So," said Ferkel, "we visit the stick house, and we talk to the neighbors. That's the detective way!"

Wolfgang raised a skeptical eyebrow. "All right. Since nothing else seems to be working . . ."

They hiked over hill and down dale until they spotted Martin Pig's house of sticks, which was hard to miss. It looked like an out-of-control beaver dam with doors, and its garden, Wolfgang noted, was a disaster area. To reach it, they had to pass by the tidy white cottage of Martin's nearest neighbor.

"First, we interview whoever lives here," said Ferkel. "Maybe they heard or saw something last night."

Wolfgang bowed and swept an arm toward the home. "Lead on, O Pig Detective. This better work."

Ferkel squared his shoulders and marched up the stone walkway.

As they approached the door, the wolf's nose wrinkled. "That smell," he said. "I know that smell."

At Ferkel's knock, the door swung open to reveal a good-sized tabby cat wearing boots and a hat. "Good day, chaps," said the tabby. "And what can I do for —?"

As soon as the cat spied Wolfgang, all the hairs on its body stood straight up like a furry pincushion. "Wolf!" it hissed.

"Cat!" snarled Wolfgang. His hackles rose and his tail went stiff.

Ferkel stepped between them with arms raised. "Whoa, whoa, whoa! Time out, both of you."

A low growl rumbled from Wolfgang's throat. The cat continued to hiss. It sounded like a landslide meeting the world's largest teakettle.

The pig doffed his blue velvet cap, jumped up, and swatted Wolfgang across the nose with it. "Bad wolf!" he cried. "Settle down!"

Wolfgang blinked, his concentration broken. Had a half-pint pig really bopped him on the nose?

Ferkel turned to the cat. "I apologize for my friend, Mr. . . . ?"

"Puss in Boots," the cat yowled, his gaze still glued to the wolf.

"Wolfgang doesn't know how to act in polite company," said Ferkel. "Listen, could I ask you a couple of questions?"

The tabby kept one paw on the door, ready to slam it in a second. "Only if he backs off."

"Oh, Wolfgang?" sang Ferkel sweetly.

The wolf grumbled and growled, but he took

several steps away from the cottage. "Ask about last night," he called.

"I will," said the pig. "Mr. Boots —"

"Call me Puss," said the cat.

"Puss, then. Were you home last night?"

Slowly, the cat's fur began to settle back into place. "The early part, yes. Before midnight."

"And did you see anyone coming or going from the stick house next door?"

Puss smoothed down his whiskers. "Well, Martin Pig, of course. He left home just before sundown."

"Anyone else?" called Wolfgang.

At his rough voice, the cat's fur bristled again. "Drat!" said Puss. "Tell him to clam up, old boy. I can't do a thing with my hair if he keeps startling me like that."

"Wolfgang, please?" said Ferkel.

"Since you asked nicely." The wolf mimed zipping his lips.

Puss in Boots licked a paw and used it to slick down his shoulder fur. "Let me think. . . ." He lapped his way down a foreleg.

Wolfgang rolled his eyes.

"Ah, yes," the cat continued. "I do recall seeing someone."

The wolf's ears perked up.

"Who?" said the pig.

"Yo mama," said Puss.

"Excuse me?" said Ferkel.

"Mama Pig. She must have stopped by around eight o'clock or so."

Wolfgang's tail drooped. This wasn't the answer he'd been hoping for.

"Anyone else?" asked Ferkel.

The cat shrugged and sat down to lick his hind leg. "Not a soul. Look, I really must finish my tongue bath now, but do drop by for tea sometime — without your friend."

"Love to."

"Don't worry," Wolfgang sneered. "I've had as much cat as I can stomach." He spun on his heel and strode down the path to Martin Pig's house, with Ferkel trotting to keep up.

"So what do you think it means?" asked Ferkel.

"Three things come to mind," said Wolfgang as they began searching around the stick house for clues. "First, your mother dropped by to see Martin, found nobody home, and left without noticing the place had been trashed."

"That makes sense." Ferkel poked through some bushes.

"Second, your mother came and trashed your brother's house."

Ferkel frowned. "That makes no sense."

"And third," said the wolf, pausing to sniff around the front of the house, "your new kitty-cat pal is either lying or too dim-witted to spot the culprit."

Ferkel cocked his head. "I think you're jealous that I hit it off with Puss."

"Jealous of that hair-ball hacker? That'll be the day."

Wolfgang rattled the locked doorknob, peered through the window, and sniffed deeply. "Double-dog-dang it!"

"What?" asked Ferkel, rising on tiptoe to look through the glass.

The wolf sneezed. "Just as I feared. Your neat-freak mother beat us here. The whole place stinks of nothing but ammonia and pig."

Wolfgang slumped onto the front steps and put his head in his paws. He might live in Fairylandia, but it was starting to seem like there'd be no happily ever after for the Big Bad Wolf.

And still the sun sank lower. His jail cell beckoned.

CHAPTER 8

In which things get buttery

Things looked so bad, Wolfgang felt like howling a mournful howl. But he was, after all, the Big Bad Wolf, with a big bad reputation to uphold, so he contented himself with a grumpy growl.

Ferkel sat down beside him. "Something wrong?"

"Really?" The wolf shot him a sarcastic look. "What makes you say that? Just because in two hours I'll be locked up for good, and we've got only the slimmest leads?"

"Cheer up!" said Ferkel. "It could always be worse."

"How?"

"There could be *no* time left and *no* leads at all."

Wolfgang shook his shaggy head. "You're such a comfort."

Ferkel beamed. "Thanks, I try. Look, the point is, we still have two hours left to crack this case."

"So what do you suggest?" said Wolfgang.

"We dash over and ask my mama why she visited last night, dash over and see if the straw house has been cleaned yet, then run and interview Cinderella," said Ferkel. "Did you know she used to go out with my brother Dieter?"

The wolf winced at the thought. "Thanks for that image. Anyway, we don't have enough time to do it all."

"So, what, then?"

Wolfgang stood. "We split up. You take your mom, I take Cinderella."

"And the straw house?" asked Ferkel.

"Send a messenger crow when you're done," said the wolf. "If there's time, we'll meet at the straw house; if not, straight to the castle."

"This is exciting!" piped Ferkel.

"A thrill a minute," said Wolfgang drily. "Now, go!"

They trotted back down the footpath, and when they reached the road, hurried away in opposite directions.

"Go easy on Cinderella!" Ferkel called back. "Use your charm!"

"I'm a wolf!" yelled Wolfgang. "We don't do charm."

"Then use your tricksiness."

"That," muttered the wolf, "I can do."

Down the road and across the meadow Wolfgang sprinted, heading for Cinderella's fancy mansion. A word about the young woman before we meet her.

You've no doubt heard Cindy's tale — the mean stepsisters, the fairy godmother, the prince, the pumpkin. And parts of it are actually true. But the story didn't unfold quite like it does in storybooks.

For one thing, the prince's ball wasn't the first affair Cinderella had crashed. In fact, this lassie made a habit out of dropping into parties uninvited and helping herself to cookies and punch, and whatever else took her fancy. And for another thing, the whole happily-ever-after bit with the prince?

Didn't work out.

Sure, they dated a few times, but Prince Tyrone was looking for someone a bit more . . . serious to rule the kingdom with him. He broke it off with Cinderella and ended up with Princess Ingrid, a much better fit.

Still, Cindy *was* able to talk him into

building her a smallish mansion before the breakup, so it wasn't a total loss.

Loping across the fields, Wolfgang took a shortcut, and before too long, he arrived at the 'Rella Estate (for that was what Cindy called her swanky house). Its gardens were immaculate, Wolfgang noted. As he headed up the curving stone walkway to the many-towered structure, the wolf smelled the buttery odor of . . . butter. He followed his nose and poked his head around the side of the mansion.

Just outside the kitchen door, Cinderella stood over her youngest stepsister, Prunella, who was grinding away at a churn.

"That's it," said Cindy. "Put some, like, elbow grease into it. I want croissants, and croissants need butter!"

"Listen to Miss Bossy," muttered her sister.

Cinderella gestured at the driveway. "Hey, anytime you want to leave . . ." She frowned when she spotted Wolfgang approaching. "Who's that? One of your boyfriends?"

Prunella arched an eyebrow. "Unlike some girls, I don't date forest creatures."

The wolf raised his paw in what he hoped was a friendly wave. "Hello, ladies!" He made an extra effort not to flash his fangs when he smiled. "Lovely day, eh?"

Cinderella and her sister traded a nervous glance. "Um, yeah, whatever," said Cindy.

"Spare a minute for a brief chat?" asked Wolfgang, doing his best to sound like one of those fancy-pants courtiers at the castle.

"Whatever you're selling, we don't need any," said Prunella, gathering up her churn.

"And we've got to get the butter into the, um,

butter thingy," said Cinderella, pretending to help her.

The wolf ignored their words and leaned on the doorframe. Prunella shrank away from him.

"I found this in your driveway," he said, producing the brown and red head scarf. "Did one of you lovely ladies drop it?"

"As if," said Cinderella. "That style is so, like, Middle Ages — I wouldn't be caught dead in it."

Wolfgang was undaunted. "Seen much of Dieter Pig lately?" he asked.

"Dieter?" said Cindy. "He's, like, ancient history."

"Word around the forest is that you parted on bad terms," said Wolfgang.

"Duh," said Cinderella. "I dumped his corn-fed butt."

"Oh." That wasn't what the wolf had been hoping to hear, but he pressed onward. "And isn't it true that when he got a new girlfriend, you went insanely jealous?"

Cindy frowned. "Me? I've already had, like, three other boyfriends since Dieter."

A bit desperately, Wolfgang continued, "Jealous enough to trash his house and his brothers' houses, too? Admit it! You did it!"

For a moment, Cinderella stared at him, wide-eyed. *This is it*, thought the wolf, *she's going to confess.*

And then Cindy threw back her head and burst into peals of laughter.

Wolfgang sighed.

"Trashed his — *ha, ha, ha!* — house?" chortled Cinderella. "That loser? Mister, you are too — *hoo, hoo!* — funny."

"So that's a no, then?" said Wolfgang miserably.

That triggered another Cinderella laugh attack, and this time Prunella joined in. Shaking their heads and wiping away tears, they lugged the butter churn inside and slammed the door in Wolfgang's face. He slumped.

Great. Just great.

Eighty minutes left, and the wolf was fresh out of suspects.

CHAPTER 9

In which a wolf gets knocked on the noggin

Wolfgang stumbled back down the driveway, visions of cold porridge filling his mind. He shook his head. This was no time to wimp out. Maybe he should review his suspects and compare them or something?

For the first time, the wolf wished that Ferkel

was there. Somehow the little pig had a knack for all that detective-y stuff, though Wolfgang would never admit that to his face.

As if summoned by his thought, the *caw-caw* of a messenger crow broke the late afternoon stillness. Black wings flapped, and the bird landed on a nearby oak branch.

"Message for wolf!" it croaked.

"Give me that!" Wolfgang made a grab for the scroll tied to the crow's leg. The bird half-hopped, half-flew to a higher branch, just out of reach.

"Money first," it said.

Wolfgang grumbled, but he dug some change from his vest pocket and held it out.

The crow swooped down, snatching the coins in its beak.

"Hey, my message!" cried Wolfgang.

As it flew off, the bird shook a leg, and the scroll fluttered down into a briar bush.

"Terrific," growled the wolf.

A few scratches and scrapes later, he retrieved the message and unfolded it. In loopy handwriting, the scroll read:

Big news! Meet me at the straw house, and I'll tell you.

— F

"Why couldn't he tell me in the note?" the wolf groused. But he slipped the message into his pocket and set off at a steady lope for the straw house. At long last, he was catching a break!

Down the road and over the creek he flew, hope making his steps lighter. Finally, Wolfgang rounded the bend and spotted it dead ahead: Hans Pig's straw house. Although it looked a bit like a haystack with windows and fancy trim, he'd never been happier to see anything in his life. Panting heavily, he trotted up to the front door. It was unlocked — yes!

The wolf turned the knob and stepped inside.

Fa-WHISH!

A thick, iron-braided rope closed around his ankle, and . . .

Fa-WHOOSH!

The trap whipped his leg up toward the ceiling, causing Wolfgang to crack his head on the oaken floor.

Stars wheeled, and suddenly everything went dark.

*   *   *

When the wolf came to, he was dangling upside down by one leg and swaying back and forth like a clock pendulum. An actual clock ticked away the minutes somewhere in the house:

Ticktock, ticktock.

Trapped.

He was trapped like a bunny in a snare, and there were only — Wolfgang cocked an eye toward the clock — fifty minutes left until he must face the prince.

His head throbbed.

His ankle hurt.

And if he didn't show up in time and reveal the culprit, he would be locked up until he was a very, very old wolf.

Wolfgang moaned. He tried to climb his own body and gnaw through the loop that

gripped his leg. The strands held. He tried swinging back and forth to catch the rope that suspended him, but all that earned him was serious dizziness.

He stopped, feeling it was best not to barf upside down.

Ticktock, ticktock.

A deep despair welled up (or down) in him. His eyes got misty. Who cared about a big bad reputation at a time like this? If ever there was an occasion for a wolf to howl, this was it.

"Ah-wooooo!" he bayed in misery. "Ah-ah-ahwoooooo!"

Wolfgang howled until he was all howled out.

But no one heard.

No one came.

After quite a few minutes of this, Wolfgang began to take a dull interest in the interior of the straw house. After all, it would be the last home he'd ever visit, outside of the dungeon.

Unlike the other two pigs' houses, it hadn't yet been cleaned. Chairs sprawled on their sides, cornflakes littered the front room, and bits of broken plates and jars lay here and there. Almost directly beneath the wolf, a small painting of Hans Pig with a pretty young sow had been viciously sliced in half.

What a mess.

It looked like Wolfgang's own house after a really good party. The whole place was a disaster area. Wait a second — not the whole place. A painting of Mama Pig still hung, perfect and intact, on one wall. And opposite the portrait,

Wolfgang noted, hung a cabinet full of Hans's fancy china, and not a cup or plate was out of place.

Odd.

Wolfgang felt a little prickle race along his spine, like he was getting a bad attack of fleas — or an idea. He took a deep sniff, hoping to catch the culprit's scent in the dusty air. He smelled cornflakes, dirty dishes, the spilled contents of the trash can, filthy clothes, and pig. Lots of pig.

But not a whiff of whoever had done this.

"Double-dog dang it!" Wolfgang cursed.

"Something wrong?" squeaked a high voice.

The wolf raised his head to see a small pig standing on the threshold.

"Ferkel?"

"I came as soon as I heard your howl," said the pig. "My mother gave me ever so many chores, but I left right in the middle of organizing the firewood logs by size."

"Never mind that," said the wolf. "Get me down from here."

"Right away!"

In flashes, as Wolfgang spun slowly, he saw: Ferkel finding a kitchen knife in the mess on the floor, Ferkel approaching the wall where the trap's rope was anchored, and Ferkel —

"Wait!" cried the wolf. "Don't just —"

The pig cut the rope.

BONK! Wolfgang landed right on his head.

"Owww!" he groaned. Now his earlier bump had a bump of its own.

The wolf lurched to his feet. "Come on!"

"To the castle?" said Ferkel.

"To the castle," said Wolfgang. "I just might know who did it, but I need your help to figure it out."

"Really?" said Ferkel with a grin. "I thought you'd never ask."

CHAPTER 10

In which all is revealed

The throne room was packed. Word had spread that the Big Bad Wolf was about to get his just deserts, and it seemed like half of Fairylandia had turned up to watch the fun.

Besides the prince and princess, their guards, and the Pig family, there were all the lords and ladies, half of the maids a-milking, three pipers piping, two drummers drumming, several swans (not swimming), Jack, Goldilocks, Cinderella, and someone's mangy dingo.

"Wow," muttered Ferkel when they walked in. "Full house."

"The better to hear us with," said Wolfgang, his eyes glinting.

Bam! Bam! Bam! Captain Kreplach pounded the butt of his pike on the floor.

"Right, then!" he shouted. "Everyone, pipe down!" He glared at some tardy noisemakers. "You too, pipers."

The room fell silent.

"Wolf," said Prince Tyrone. "You are accused of vandalizing the Three Little Pigs' houses and stealing their food. Do you have anything to say before we lock you up for the rest of your rotten life?"

"I sure do," said Wolfgang.

The prince rolled his eyes. "Very well. Keep it brief."

Wolfgang gazed around the room at all the blood-hungry expressions, coming last of all to Ferkel, who gave him a thumbs-up. "You all think I'm a killer," the wolf told the crowd. "A dirty, low-down chicken plucker and all-around bad guy."

"Well, duh!" called someone. "That's 'cause you are!" People chuckled.

Gritting his teeth, Wolfgang continued, "Yes, it's true, I may have stolen a chicken or two."

"Or twenty!" called someone else. The prince glared, and finally the chuckles subsided.

"But this time," said Wolfgang, "you've got the wrong wolf. I didn't do it."

A wave of jeers and catcalls swept the room. Captain Kreplach pounded his pike on the floor and bellowed, "Shut your pieholes, you cretins!" until all the pieholes were shut.

"And with the help of my friend Ferkel," Wolfgang said, "I can prove who did it."

Up until now, the Three Little Pigs and their mother had looked fat and sassy, not a care in the world. But when she heard this, Mama Pig frowned.

"Together, Ferkel and I talked to all the likely suspects — Jack, Goldilocks, Cinderella, Hansel and Gretel, and so on," said the wolf.

"And it was *fun!*" Ferkel burbled. At a glance from Wolfgang, he settled down.

"But there was something wrong with nearly every one," the wolf continued.

The little pig couldn't contain himself. "Some of them had alibis, some had no motive — that's the reason you do it — and some of them" — here, he smiled at Cinderella — "just weren't bright enough to pull it off."

She smiled back, then asked the man next to her, "What does he mean?"

Wolfgang paced the cold marble floor. "The problem was, we hadn't put all the facts together properly, like a real detective would have."

"A what?" said Captain Kreplach.

"You know . . ." The wolf waved his paw. "A figure-outer of things."

"So here's what we figured out," Ferkel said, joining the pacing. "Fact one: The vandal left this head scarf behind." He flourished the red and brown scarf.

"Fact two," said the wolf, "it smelled like pig."

"Fact three: In the straw house, only the good china and the picture of my mama were undamaged," said Ferkel.

"Fact four: The whole place smelled like pig." Wolfgang furtively swiped away a strand of drool.

"Fact five," said Ferkel, "someone pretending to be me sent a message to Wolfgang, luring him into a trap."

"Ooh," said the crowd.

The wolf scowled. "And it really, really hurt my ankle. In fact —"

"Is this nearly over?" the prince interrupted. "I've got a feast waiting."

Ferkel held up his hooves. "Almost there, Your Highness."

"Fact six," said Wolfgang, "Mama Pig visited her son Martin's house last night while he was away."

"Oh?" said the crowd.

Mama Pig's eyes shifted back and forth, and she wiped her neck with a handkerchief.

Ferkel turned to face her. "And last of all, fact seven: Mama, you've been really happy today, now that all of your sons are back in your house."

She beamed at him. "Well, that's true. It's so good to have my boys at home."

"Why'd you do it, Mama?" asked Ferkel softly. "Why'd you trash my brothers' houses?"

"I — I — I . . ." A faint red tinge came to her

pink cheeks. Her gaze flicked from Ferkel, to the wolf, to the prince, to her sons.

The whole room leaned forward.

"I just wanted my piglets back home," said Mama Pig. "Is that such a crime, for a mother to love her sons?"

"Aww," said the crowd.

"*That's* not a crime," said Wolfgang. "But I'm pretty sure breaking and entering, thievery and vandalism, framing someone, and illegally trapping a wolf are."

Captain Kreplach nodded. "He's got you there, luv."

The prince sighed. "Oh, all right. Captain, lock her up in the dungeon for a hundred years, there's a good fellow."

Two burly guards stepped forward.

The Three Little Pigs went pale. "Wait, Sire!" cried Dieter.

Prince Tyrone glowered. "What did I say about that 'Sire' stuff?"

"Sorry, Your, um, Awesomeness?" said Dieter. "But what if we don't press charges? Is it still a crime, then?"

The prince stroked his handsome jaw and looked a question at Captain Kreplach, who shrugged. "No, I suppose not. If the wronged piggies — er, parties — don't press charges, and the wolf doesn't mind" — he glanced at Wolfgang, who also shrugged — "then she can go free."

The Three Little Pigs clapped and laughed and crowded around their mother. Even Ferkel got in on the group hug.

"But next time you want to see them," cried Prince Tyrone over the hubbub, "just invite your sons to dinner."

"Mmm, dinner," muttered the wolf at the thought of all those pork chops.

CHAPTER 11

In which everyone goes happy-ever-aftering

Outside the throne room, Captain Kreplach caught up with Wolfgang and offered his hand. "No hard feelin's, mate. It was an honest mistake."

"*Honest?*" said the wolf.

"Well, you are Public Enemy Number One and all," said the captain. "You gots to admit, you make a dandy suspect, Mr. Big Bad — er, Wolf."

The wolf sighed and shook his hand.

"A man can admit when he's made a mistake," said Captain Kreplach. "Course, that don't mean I won't catch you next time."

The wolf smiled a toothy smile. "You're welcome to try."

The commander flinched at the sight of all those fangs and edged away. "Right, then," he muttered. "Gotta get goin', lots of stuff to guard."

"Ta-ta, Captain," said Wolfgang.

The Pig family stepped into the hallway, chattering happily. When Ferkel spotted the wolf, he broke away from his brothers and trotted over.

"That was quite a case," said the pig.

"*You're* quite a case," said the wolf. "But I couldn't have done it without you."

Ferkel blushed. "Aw, thanks. And thanks for what you've done for my reputation."

Wolfgang scratched his head. "What do you mean? You've been seen hanging around with Public Enemy Number One, a dirty, low-down chicken plucker."

"Exactly," said the pig. "And that's done wonders for my reputation. Partners, Wolfie?"

"I'm not a detective, I'm a gardener. And don't call me —" But before he could finish, Jack stumped over to them on his crutches.

"Hullo, you two," said Jack. "Jolly well done! Of all the big bads, you're the baddest!"

The wolf and pig thanked him.

"Hey, listen," said Jack. "If you're not too busy, I wonder if you might take on a new case."

Wolfgang's ears flicked in surprise. "New case?" he said. "But we're not —"

"Go on," said Ferkel.

Jack glanced from side to side. "See, here's the thing: Someone stole Brutus the Giant's golden goose, and he thinks it was me. I need you two to clear my name and catch the real thief, just like you did today."

"But we —" Wolfgang tried again.

"Would love to take your case," said Ferkel. "For four gold pieces, on retainer."

At the sight of the coins, the wolf shut his mouth. Gardening could wait.

"All right, then," said Jack, pressing them into Wolfgang's grip. "Come 'round tomorrow, and I'll give you all the details."

Wordlessly, Wolfgang watched the lad clomp away on his crutches. His gaze was thoughtful.

"First thing," said Ferkel, "we've got to come up with a name for our detective business."

Wolfgang raised an eyebrow. "How does the Big Bad Detective Agency sound to you?"

Ferkel grinned. "Like the start of a beautiful partnership."